Fredericksburg VA 22401
1201 Caroline Street

ELSINA'S CLOUDS

Jeanette Winter

FRANCES FOSTER BOOKS
FARRAR, STRAUS AND GIROUX
NEW YORK

Fredericksburg VA 22401
1201 Caroline Street

for Barbara Beckmann

Copyright © 2004 by Jeanette Winter
All rights reserved
Distributed in Canada by Douglas & McIntyre Ltd.
Color separations by Hong Kong Scanner Arts
Printed and bound in the United States of America by Berryville Graphics
Designed by Jeanette Winter
Font designed by Judythe Sieck
First edition, 2004
1 3 5 7 9 10 8 6 4 2

Library of Congress Cataloging-in-Publication Data
Winter, Jeanette.
    Elsina's clouds / Jeanette Winter.— 1st ed.
        p.   cm.
    Summary: In South Africa, a Basotho girl paints designs on her
house as a prayer to the ancestors for rain.
    ISBN 0-374-32118-3
    [1. Rain and rainfall—Fiction.   2. House painting—Fiction.   3. Sotho
(African people)—Fiction.   4. South Africa—Fiction.]   I. Title.

PZ7.W7547 El 2004
[E]—dc21

                                                        2002029704

Basotho women of southern Africa
have painted their houses for hundreds of years.
The designs are a prayer to the
ancestors for rain.

I paint when the sun
peeks over the mountain.
I paint when the sun
sits high in the blue.
I paint until the colors
turn to darkness.

Then one night the clouds part and drift away.

At daybreak
I see blue again.

The sorghum in Mama's field blossoms.
Papa's goats grow fat.
My brother comes into the world.
And I paint.

We wait.

But when the rain clouds leave
I take my paint
and cover the walls again.

The ancestors listen.